HOLD THAT THOUGHT, MILTON!

Withdrawn from Stock
Dublin City Public Libraries

D0452558

To Michael –
who is full of thoughts that make us all more thoughtful
L.R.L

For Willow aka Contessa Von Huffington
R.C.

This edition published by Parragon Books Ltd in 2014

Parragon Books Ltd
Chartist House
15–17 Trim Street
Bath BA1 1HA, UK

www.parragon.com

Published by arrangement with Gullane Children's Books

Text © Linda Ravin Lodding 2013
Illustrations © Ross Collins 2013

All rights reserved. No part of this publication may be reproduced, stored in a retrieval
system or transmitted, in any form or by any means, electronic, mechanical, photocopying,
recording or otherwise, without the prior permission of the copyright holder.

ISBN 978-1-4723-3199-1

Printed in China

HOLD THAT THOUGHT, MILTON!

LINDA RAVIN LODDING
AND
ROSS COLLINS

PaRRagon
Bath • New York • Singapore • Hong Kong • Cologne • Delhi
Melbourne • Amsterdam • Johannesburg • Shenzhen

Milton had many things on his mind and a lot to say.
The trouble was he couldn't get anyone to listen.

"Do all frogs have twenty-three warts like my frog Burp?"

Milton asked his mother.

Leabharlanna Poibli Chathair Baile Átha Cliath

Dublin City Public Libraries

"Hold that thought, Milton," she said.

"I'm busy sewing water lilies
onto Aunt Lulu's wedding dress.
She's having a rainforest theme."

"Dad, if the earth is spinning, why doesn't everyone fly off?"

"Hold that thought, Milt-o," Dad said. "I'm rehearsing my wedding tango."

Leabharlanna Poibli Chathair Baile Átha Cliath

Dublin City Public Libraries

Then, the day before Aunt Lulu's wedding,
something mind-boggling happened.
It started...

When Burp
disappeared.

"Gramps," Milton began, **"could Burp survive in Grammy's..."**

"Hold that thought, Milty," said Gramps. "I need to practise the tuba for The Wedding March."

"**Mum,**" asked Milton, "**have you seen...**"

"**Hold that thought, Milton dear.** I'm watering the Coccoloba for Aunt Lulu's bouquet."

"**Spike,**" pleaded Milton, "**what if Burp falls into the lime jelly?**"

"Can't hear you, dude," said Milton's brother.

But it wasn't easy for Milton to hold his thoughts...

His head began to feel **tight** and his skin became **itchy**...

Suddenly,
his hair
spiked up
like a
toilet brush

and his
ears turned a

shocking
shade of
GREEN!

Milton's mother gasped,
"Your ears! They're GREEN!"
And she called for Doctor Czechup.

Milton cradled his beloved Burp.

"Why didn't you tell us Burp was lost?"
asked Dad.

"I tried to tell," said Milton,
"but no one listened.

Sometimes I have
important things to say!"

"From now on, we're all ears," said Mother, planting a pucker on Milton's head.

Milton returned to normal.

So did the wedding...

Well, almost.

Leabharlanna Poibli Chathair Baile Átha Cliath
Dublin City Public Libraries